The Hidden Cave

by RUTH CHEW

Illustrated by the author

SCHOLASTIC BOOK SERVICES

NEW YORK • TORONTO • LONDON • AUCKLAND • SYDNEY • TOKYO

To Mark Kelton

ISBN: 0-590-06115-1

Copyright © 1973 by Ruth Chew. All rights reserved. Published by Scholastic Book Services, a division of Scholastic Magazines, Inc.

13 12 11 10 9 8 7 6 5 4 3   0 1 2 3 4/8
Printed in the U. S. A.   11

1

"ALICE, look at Freckles!" Tom grabbed his sister's arm and pointed.

It was a steaming hot day. Alice and Tom had been jumping from rock to rock in the little stream in Prospect Park. Alice stopped to look up at the bank above the stream. She could see just the fluffy tip of Freckles' tail sticking out of a tangle of vines. A moment later the tail disappeared and there was no sign of the dog at all.

Tom climbed the slippery bank to the place where Freckles had been. He pushed aside the heavy vine that hung down from a rocky ledge. "Al!" Tom was excited. "Guess what I found!"

Alice was almost two years older than Tom. It seemed to her that he was always excited about something. "You found a spotted cocker spaniel," she said. "And I hope he didn't catch the chipmunk he was chasing."

Tom got down on his hands and knees and squirmed under the vines where Freckles had disappeared. After a few squirms he too was hidden behind the vine. "Al, come on up here," he yelled. Tom's voice was still excited, but it sounded different now, sort of hollow.

Maybe she ought to look at what Tom had found. Alice was standing on a rock in the middle of the stream. She jumped to the bank. Holding on to bushes and clumps of grass, she climbed up to the patch of vines. With one hand she lifted a thick vine. It was like a curtain. Behind it Alice found the opening of a large drainage pipe.

There were rocks all around the pipe to make it look like a cave. Three rusty iron bars blocked the opening, but long ago someone had twisted one of the iron bars loose on one side.

Tom had crawled under the twisted bar. He was squatting inside the pipe. When Alice lifted the curtain of vines he grinned at her. "It's a real cave," he said.

2

ALICE was excited now too, but all she said was, "It's just an old sewer pipe. Where's Freckles?"

Tom had been so surprised to find the cave that he had forgotten the dog. Now he began to whistle.

The pipe stretched back into the hill. It was dark there. A scratching noise came from the black tunnel. The noise became louder, and Freckles came running out of the darkness. He rushed to greet the children. His tail wagged so hard that the back half of Freckles wagged along with it.

Freckles ran under the twisted bar. He jumped around Alice as if he were on springs. She gave him a pat with the hand that wasn't holding up the vine, but she kept looking into the tunnel. "I wonder where it goes."

"Let's explore it, Al." Tom crawled farther into the pipe. Alice bent down to go under the bar. She was bigger than Tom. She had to lie flat on her stomach and twist to get in. Freckles squeezed in after her.

When Alice let go of the vine it flopped down over the opening of the cave and cut out most of the light. It was cooler here than outside. The daylight sifted through layers of leaves. This part of the cave was lit with a soft green glow.

Once Alice had wiggled her way into the cave she found that there was just enough room for her to sit up. If she were any taller she'd have to lean forward.

Now Alice and Tom heard voices

outside. They were coming closer. Alice put her arm around Freckles to keep him quiet. She leaned close to the bars and peeked through the vine. Three big boys were walking along the stream. Two of them tried to push the other one into the water. He dodged them and ran up the bank on the other side. Alice and Tom sat very still until the boys were gone.

"We don't want anybody else to find this place," Alice whispered.

She heard a little scraping noise. A small flame was burning, back where Tom was sitting. "I found a book of matches on a park bench," Tom explained. "It has two whole rows of matches in it."

"We can use one row to explore the tunnel," Alice said. "Save the other row for the way back. Come on."

Tom went first into the tunnel. Alice

came after him, and Freckles followed her. They couldn't go very fast. Tom had to hold the match.

The pipe seemed to go uphill. The air was cool and damp here. Tom lit another match. In a little while they were out of sight of the opening of the cave. They crawled along for what seemed like ages.

"Can you see the end of the tunnel yet?" Alice asked.

"No," Tom said. "It's still dark up ahead. And there are only two matches left in this row."

"Try to let them burn a little longer." Alice arched her back and tried to stretch her legs.

"Ow!" Tom dropped the match. It went out. "I burned my finger."

"Does it hurt?" Alice asked.

"Sure does. What do we do now?" Tom asked.

Alice held out her hand. "Give me the matches."

"Can't," Tom said. "I've lost them."

"Hold still. Maybe they're caught in your clothes." Alice reached to grab Tom. She began to feel for the matches.

"Stop it, Al. You're tickling," Tom giggled. "Hey, get your fingers out of my mouth. Take it easy."

Alice let go of him. "Feel on the ground. They can't be far away. Let's go back the way we came. Where's Freckles?"

Alice felt the dog's cold wet nose on her hand. She hugged him. It made her feel better to know that Freckles wasn't afraid of the dark. His wagging tail banged against her knee.

Alice held on to the dog's collar, and Tom grabbed hold of Alice's pants leg. They crawled along in the darkness for a few feet. Then Alice felt something

with her free hand. It was the book of matches.

"I've found them, Tom!" Alice pulled a match out of the book and tried to strike it. The match bent. "They're wet! There's water in this pipe."

A tiny stream was trickling through the pipe. The stream seemed to be getting deeper. The water in it was flowing faster every minute. By this time Alice was really scared.

They crawled faster. The knees of their pants were wet. Freckles liked wading. He splashed the children's faces with his tail.

At last Alice saw a glimmer of green light. She let go of the dog and moved ahead on all fours. When they reached the mouth of the cave she peeked through the curtain of vines. "No wonder it's wet in here. It's pouring outside."

3

THE rain was splashing down. There was a rumble of thunder. Suddenly a bright flash of lightning lit up the cave. The children heard a loud crash. Freckles was so scared that he tried to climb into Alice's lap. Tom jumped and banged his head on the roof of the pipe. "That was close, Al."

Alice looked out again through the wet vine leaves. A huge oak tree stood on the other side of the stream. It was black and twisted with age. The lightning had knocked off one of the crooked branches and split the great trunk in half.

Alice stared at the tree. "Tom," she whispered, "look!"

Tom crawled to the mouth of the cave and looked through the leaves. Someone seemed to be curled up inside the split trunk of the old tree.

"We've got to get help." Alice lay on her stomach to crawl under the iron bar. She pushed aside the vine and crept out into the downpour.

The bank was slippery. Alice skidded down to the stream on the seat of her pants. Freckles wiggled out of the cave after her. He bounded down the slope and leaped across the rushing water. Tom followed.

Alice was in such a hurry that she just waded through the stream and headed up the bank toward the ruined tree. When she reached it she found an old man asleep in the hollow trunk. Funny, Alice thought, he's wearing a white fur coat in the middle of summer. When Alice looked closer she saw that the coat was really his hair and his beard. They were so long that they were all tangled together and seemed to be wrapped around and around the old man.

Tom had come up beside her. "Wow!" he said.

The two children and the dog stood in the pouring rain and stared. The old man opened his eyes. They were very blue and bright, not like the eyes of an old man at all.

He stretched. When he moved, the cloth of his sleeves fell apart. His bare arms were very pale, as if they hadn't been in the sunshine for a long time. All his clothes seemed to be turning to dust. It's lucky he has all that hair, Alice thought.

"Are you all right?" Tom asked the old man.

The man looked at Tom as if he couldn't understand what he said.

"Maybe he's deaf," Alice whispered.

"ARE YOU ALL RIGHT?" Tom shouted.

The old man put his hands over his ears. "Softly, lad," he said. "It will take me a little while to get used to your way of speaking, but I was always quick to learn." He spoke slowly as if he were picking the words out of the air. He didn't seem to notice the pouring rain.

Alice couldn't keep quiet any longer. "What were you doing in the tree?"

"I was enchanted," the old man said. "I have tried for more than a thousand years to break the spell."

"You're kidding," Tom said. "That tree's old, but not that old."

"It grew from the acorn of an older tree in a far-off land," the old man told him. "It took me hundreds of years to learn how to fit into an acorn." He stretched again. The rain fell on his long hair and white arms.

Alice poked Tom to make him be quiet. "Who are you?" she asked the old man.

"I am Merlin," he said. "Have you never heard of Merlin the magician?"

Alice shook her head.

Tom said, "I saw a magician on television."

"Television? Is that a new kind of magic?" Merlin asked.

"Yes, in a way," Alice said.

Merlin looked at her. "In all the years I've been shut up I've forgotten my magic. Perhaps, if I work hard, I can get some of it back. Can you help me? I need a place to stay."

Alice was sure her mother wouldn't want her to bring home a crazy old man, but there was something about him that Alice liked. She wanted to help him. He was very thin. It gave her an idea.

"I know a place where you could stay," she said, "if you're good at crawling on your stomach."

Tom understood. "She means the cave," he said. "You can live there, and we'll bring you food. Right now the cave is wet, but it's a lot drier than it is out here. Come on. We'll show you where it is."

Merlin looked interested. He stood up and began to climb out of the tree. He had to keep unhooking his hair and his beard from twigs and branches. Even though his hair was wrapped four

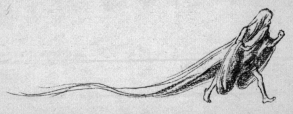

times around his body it dragged on the ground. Before he could walk without tripping, the old man had to loop his hair around one arm and his beard around the other.

Alice and Tom crossed the stream and climbed the bank on the other side. They lifted the vine to show Merlin the cave. He slipped under the bar almost as easily as Freckles could.

The dog followed him into the pipe. Then Alice and Tom squeezed in to get out of the rain. Merlin crawled farther into the pipe and lay down. It wasn't big enough for him to sit up, but he didn't seem to mind.

"My friends," he said, "you must tell me your names."

Tom was sitting near the mouth of the cave hugging Freckles. "I'm Tom Nelson," he said. "This is my sister Alice."

"Thank you for bringing me to this shelter, Tom and Alice." Merlin was trying to untangle his beard from his hair. "I'll have to do something about this."

"Would you like me to bring you a pair of scissors?" Alice asked. "And maybe Tom and I can find something for you to wear."

Merlin smiled. "My clothing does seem to be in need of a change. If it's not too much trouble, I'd like a robe of blue and gold."

Alice had been thinking of an old sweat shirt and some trousers that her father had grown too fat for. Now she noticed that the old man was wearing a ring that flashed even in the dim light of the cave. Alice wondered if it could be a diamond. She decided that the old sweat shirt wouldn't be right at all for Merlin.

4

WHEN the rain stopped, Alice and Tom left Merlin lying in the cave. He seemed quite at home there.

"He's a nice old guy," Tom said, "but I don't believe that stuff about his being enchanted."

Alice stooped to put the leash on Freckles. "How else could his hair grow so long?"

The grass was wet and the trees dripped. Alice and Tom made their way to one of the gates of the park.

They lived in an old brownstone house nearby. Both their parents were away at work all day. Alice had a key to the front door.

When Alice walked into the house she remembered that her mother had asked her to put the laundry into the washing machine. She went upstairs to get the clothes out of the hamper.

Alice used her bedspread to wrap the laundry in. The white spread still had peanut butter and jelly on it from the picnic she and Tom had in her room on a rainy day.

Alice's new blue jeans were wet and muddy from her slide down the bank by the stream. She decided to wash them too.

She changed into an old pair of pants and carried the laundry down to the basement. Alice stuffed all the clothes into the washing machine. She added the soap, turned on the machine, and went to look for Tom.

She found him in the kitchen. He was looking into the refrigerator. "What do you suppose we ought to feed the old guy?" Tom took out a container of milk and filled a glass for himself.

Alice poured some dog chow into Freckles' dish. She pulled a banana from the bunch on the table and began to peel it. "Cheese ought to be a good thing," she said. "And there's half a loaf of bread." She shut the refrigerator door. "Would he like cherry soda?"

By the time Alice and Tom had finished lunch the washing machine had stopped. "Tom," Alice said, "would you put the laundry into the dryer? I have to look for some clothes to give Merlin."

"There's a lot of old stuff in that cedar chest in my room," Tom told her.

Alice went to Tom's bedroom. She opened the chest. Most of the things in it were old clothes of hers or Tom's. There was a baggy pair of pajamas that belonged to Alice's father, but they were green with tan stripes. Merlin wanted blue and gold.

Underneath everything in the chest Alice saw something shining. She reached in and pulled out a pair of gold curtain tie-backs. They were like two short ropes. Alice thought they might be knotted together to make a belt.

Tom came into the room. "Did you find anything?"

Alice held up the tie-backs.

"I guess I ought to tell you the laundry looks awful," Tom said. "What did you put in it that ran blue all over everything?"

Alice thought for a moment. "My blue jeans," she said. "They've never been washed before." Alice dropped the tie-backs on the floor and ran to look at the laundry.

The first thing she pulled out of the dryer was the bedspread. It had been dyed a beautiful pale blue.

5

MRS. Nelson came home early. "My boss gave everybody in the office the afternoon off," she told the children. "The air-conditioner broke down, and it was too hot to work."

Tom and Alice were getting ready to go back to the park. Their mother had other plans for them. "Tom," she said, "run to the hardware store. I need a new sponge mop."

When Mrs. Nelson saw the laundry she filled the washing machine and poured a cup of bleach into the water.

"Take the white things out of the dryer, Alice, and let them soak in the washing machine for a while. And next time remember to wash the colored clothes separately."

Alice waited until her mother had gone upstairs. Then she took all the white things except the bedspread out of the dryer and put them back into the washing machine.

Tom came back from the hardware store. Mrs. Nelson asked him to move the chairs and table out of the kitchen. She was going to wash the floor. Alice tried to sneak through the kitchen, but her mother saw her. "Here's a duster, Alice. See if you can dust the books in the living-room bookcase." When Mrs. Nelson cleaned house everybody had to help.

Alice began to take each book out of the bookcase and dust it before putting it back. She got almost all the way through the top shelf when she came to a big red book with gold letters on it. *KING ARTHUR*, Alice read. The book fell open on the floor. Alice was about to close it when she saw a picture of an old man in a long robe. Under the picture was printed the one word MERLIN.

When Mrs. Nelson finished washing and waxing the kitchen floor she came into the living room. Alice was sitting cross-legged on the floor in front of the bookcase reading the big red book.

Her mother was tired and cross. She took the book away from Alice. "This is not the time to read," she said. "Finish your dusting."

Alice picked up the dust cloth and went back to work, but she kept thinking of what she had read. Merlin had

been a very wise man long ago. He had been the friend of kings. It was sad that now he was just a funny old man with a long beard.

Mr. Nelson came home before Alice finished dusting. There was no time to go back to the park before supper.

After the dishes were washed and put away, Alice went down into the basement and took the bedspread out of the dryer. She hurried upstairs with it.

Alice searched all through her desk but she couldn't find what she wanted. She went to look for Tom. He was in his room trying to teach Freckles to fetch a ball.

"Have you seen my box of gold paper stars?" Alice asked Tom.

"It's over there on the windowsill," Tom said. "I was going to stick some of them on my ceiling, but I have to get the ladder first. Freckles, give me that ball."

"You know Mother won't like you sticking stars on your ceiling," Alice said. "Besides, they're my stars, and I have something better to do with them." Alice took the box off the windowsill. She went back to her own room.

Tom was curious. He left Freckles hiding under his bed with the ball and went to see what Alice was up to.

Alice had put the spread back on her bed. Now she started licking the gold paper stars and sticking them here and there on the spread.

"What makes you think Mom will approve of *that*?" Tom asked.

Alice jumped. Tom had been so quiet that she didn't know he was standing in her doorway. She pulled Tom into the room and shut the door. "What matters is," she whispered, "will Merlin approve?"

Tom stared at her. "You're going to use your bedspread for a robe for that nutty old guy?"

"He's not a nutty old guy." Alice told Tom what she had read in *KING ARTHUR*. "I can't give him just anything for a robe," she finished.

Tom looked worried. "I wonder if he's hungry. If he really spent all that time in the tree he ought to be starving."

Alice looked out of her window. A full moon was coming up over the row of houses behind theirs. "Tom," she said, "suppose we went to see him *tonight*?"

Mr. Nelson banged on Alice's door. "Is Tom in there? It's his bedtime."

"Go to bed, Tom," Alice whispered. "We'll sneak out later."

6

THE moon was high over the trees in the park. Old lamp posts stood here and there along the paths. Long ago people often walked in Prospect Park at night. Now Alice and Tom were the only ones there.

They hurried across the meadow toward the stream. Here it was very dark. The lamp posts were far apart. "We should have brought Freckles," Alice said.

Tom stared hard at the shadows under the trees. He began to remember the stories he had heard of terrible things that happened in the park at night. "I wish we'd brought a flash-light."

Alice fished in her pants pocket and pulled out the thick stump of a candle. "I found this in the kitchen drawer," she said.

"Did you bring matches?" Tom asked.

Alice took a handful of wooden kitchen matches out of her pocket.

Tom was carrying a paper bag with bread and cheese and bananas in it. Alice had folded her bedspread around the curtain tie-backs. She carried it under one arm.

The ground was still soggy from the rainstorm. It squelched beneath their sneakers. They followed a walk that led under an old stone bridge. It was so black there that Alice lit the candle. The flickering light made the shadows look even more scary.

On the other side of the bridge they climbed a bank and went along a path

that overlooked the stream. The moonlight glinted on the water. Alice blew
out the candle.

"We ought to be coming to the cave
soon," Tom said.

Alice pointed. "There's the big tree."

The huge split trunk seemed even
blacker and more twisted in the moonlight. As the children came closer they
saw that the hollow inside the tree
gleamed faintly.

Tom stared at it. "Maybe the old guy
was telling the truth. It sure is a strange
tree."

Alice led the way down the slippery
bank and across the stream. She climbed
the bank on the other side until she
reached the curtain of vines. Then she
lit the candle again.

"Who's there?" a voice called from
the cave.

"It's Tom and Alice." Tom's voice sounded loud in the stillness. "We brought you something to eat."

The vine leaves moved. A thin white form slid out from under them. Merlin stood up. He was taller than the children remembered. With his white hair and beard streaming down, he looked like a ghost in the moonlight.

"My thanks," he said. "You have noble hearts." He sat on a rock to eat. The bread and cheese, he said, was different from what he was used to. He didn't seem to like it, but he was charmed by the wrappings on the food. He held the clear plastic up to gaze through it at the moon.

And the bananas were new to him. The children had to show how him to peel them.

When the meal was over Alice put

the folded bedspread on a rock and handed Merlin a comb. He began to comb his hair and beard.

It took a long time to get out all the tangles. Alice had to help him. Tom held the candle. At last the long white hair was combed. It stretched down the bank and coiled in a shining silver heap at the edge of the stream.

Alice took a small pair of scissors out of her pocket. "It's so beautiful," she said, looking at the streaming white hair. "Why don't we braid it before we cut it off? Then you could keep it."

Merlin nodded. "Do you think you could do it?"

"If Tom helps me," Alice said.

Merlin held the candle. The two children started to work. Braiding the old man's beard and hair was like doing a maypole dance up and down the hill above the stream.

When they were finished, Alice cut Merlin's hair at shoulder length and his beard at his waist. She knotted the ends of the braids.

Alice found the bedspread where she had left it on the rock. She unrolled it and took out the curtain tie-backs. Then she draped the bedspread over the magician's bare shoulders. Merlin wrapped it around himself as if he were an Indian in a blanket.

Alice tied the curtain tie-backs together to make a belt and cut two slits in the beadspread for armholes.

Merlin admired his robe. The paper stars shone in the candlelight, and the fringe brushed softly against the old man's ankles. "You have done well, my friend," he said.

Alice felt very proud.

7

IT was long after midnight when Alice and Tom opened their front door and crept upstairs to bed. Alice was so excited that she couldn't get to sleep for a while. It seemed as if she had just closed her eyes when she heard her mother calling. "Good morning, Alice. Time to get up."

Alice rolled out of bed.

"It's going to be another scorcher," Mrs. Nelson was saying. "Why don't you and Tom set up the wading pool in the backyard?"

Alice blinked at the bright sunlight coming through her open window. Everything that had happened last night seemed faraway and unreal. Had she dreamed it?

During breakfast Mr. Nelson noticed that Tom was much more quiet than usual. "Don't you feel well, Tom?"

Tom looked up from his bowl of cereal. "I feel fine, Dad." Then he asked, "Did you know about bananas when you were a boy?"

"What do you mean, 'know about bananas'?" his father demanded.

"Did you know how to peel them?" Tom asked.

"Of course. Are you sure you feel well, Tom?"

When Mr. and Mrs. Nelson had gone off to work, Alice and Tom washed the breakfast dishes and made the beds. "I wonder what Merlin would like for breakfast," Alice said.

She looked in the kitchen cabinet and took out a little box of cornflakes. "He could eat right out of this box." Alice poured some milk into an empty peanut butter jar and shoved a spoon into her pocket.

Then she put the leash on Freckles. "Come on, Tom." The two children went out of the house and headed for the park. Freckles bounded along beside them.

After they had crossed the road that wound through the park and were at the edge of the meadow, Alice took off Freckles' leash. The dog dashed around and around Alice and Tom. Then he streaked across the meadow toward the stream. The children followed.

They found Merlin sitting in a swing. He had tied the ropes made from his hair and his beard to the branch of a tall sycamore tree. The seat of the swing was a piece from the old oak tree. The fringes of the blue robe fluttered as the old man swung back and forth. When he saw the children he let the swing come to a stop.

"Good morning, Merlin," Tom called. "Are you ready for breakfast?"

Merlin thought the cornflakes were little dry leaves. Tom and Alice had a hard time getting him to try them. Alice poured milk into the cornflakes box and handed the spoon to the magician.

After two bites Merlin decided that he could eat the little brown leaves after all. And when he had finished the box he wiped the milk from his snowy moustache with the back of his hand. "Truly," he said, "that was a good meal."

Alice and Tom took turns swinging.

The ropes were so long that they could swing right across the stream.

While Tom was pumping to make the swing go higher, Alice stood near the cave and talked to the magician. "Why did you make the swing?"

The old man smiled. "Ah, you think only children love swings. I find them good for the mind. When my body soars up from the ground I can think more clearly."

Alice remembered the stories in *KING ARTHUR* of all the wonderful things Merlin used to do: "Has it helped you remember your magic?" she asked.

"It has made me want to know more about this place where I find myself. What is at the end of the tunnel?" Merlin pointed to the cave.

Alice told him how she and Tom had tried to explore the cave. The magician listened until she had finished. "We need a torch." He picked up a twisted pine branch from the ground. "This would do if only we had a fire."

Alice took a match out of her pocket and struck it on a rock. Merlin held the match to the pine branch. It smoked for a few moments and then burst into flame.

Tom jumped off the swing. He scrambled up the rocky bank. "What's going on, Al?"

"We're going to explore the tunnel again." Alice lifted the vines from the mouth of the cave.

Merlin gave Alice the torch. He crawled into the drainpipe. Then he reached through the bars for the torch.

Alice and Tom went after the magician into the cave. The dog followed them.

The water from yesterday's rain was gone from the pipe. Merlin wrapped the bedspread around himself and crawled down the tunnel. He held the torch in one hand and moved forward on his elbows. Alice and Tom were surprised at how fast he went. They had a hard time keeping up with him.

The torch gave more light than the matches they had used yesterday. But it was much smokier. Alice's eyes began to sting. Merlin was still crawling ahead of her through the tunnel. "Next time we'd better bring a flashlight," she told Tom. "What happened to the one Daddy gave you last Christmas?"

"The batteries leaked all over it." Tom coughed. "This smoke is awful."

They crawled on and on through the smoky pipe. Suddenly Merlin stopped. "There's light up ahead," he said. The magician blew out the torch.

8

MERLIN left the torch behind and they all crawled out of the pipe.

They found themselves on a stairway inside a building. Merlin looked around. "There is magic here. I can smell it."

Alice looked behind her. "Tom," she whispered, "he's right. There is magic here. The pipe is gone!"

A door banged, and a man came down the stairs. "Hey, you kids," he said, "what makes you think you can bring a dog into the public library?"

Tom ran up the stairs and opened the door at the top. He looked in and then came back down. "It's the library all right, Al," he said. "I'd better take Freckles outside. Give me the leash. I'll wait for you in front of the building."

Merlin's blue eyes shone. "A library!" he said. "In books I can find the magic I have forgotten."

Alice took the magician to the reference room. She wondered what people would say when they saw him.

The woman at the information desk was talking to a young man. His hair was shaved on top, but in back it was gathered into a pigtail. There was a white streak painted down his nose. He wore an orange-colored garment that was looped between his legs.

Nearby two tall young men with curly beards and bare feet were looking at the books on the shelves. No one seemed to notice the old man with the white beard and the starry robe.

Alice asked the woman at the desk if there were any books on magic in the library. To her surprise the woman pointed to a set of shelves near the windows. "You'll find books on the occult and the supernatural over there."

Merlin took a look at the books. One on the second shelf caught his eye. It was old and dog-eared. The magician sat down at a long table and opened the book. He leafed quickly through it. Near the end he started to read a chapter. Alice peeked over his shoulder. She couldn't understand the words Merlin was reading. They weren't like anything she'd ever seen before.

The magician finished reading the chapter. Then he read it again. He did this three times. At last he shut the book. "I'm beginning to remember how it's done," he said to Alice.

Alice put the book back on the shelf where it belonged. She and Merlin went downstairs and out of the main door of the library. Tom and Freckles were waiting for them.

9

OUTSIDE the library Merlin stared at the cars and trucks rushing by. When the traffic light changed, Alice and Tom started to cross the street. "Hurry, Merlin," Tom said.

Alice held the old man's hand and pulled him across the street to the park on the other side.

"Hey, Al," Tom said. "The zoo is just down the street. Maybe Merlin would like to see the animals. There's a short-cut back to the stream from the rear gate of the zoo."

The magician and the children walked down Flatbush Avenue toward the zoo. Merlin kept looking at the traffic. "There's a strange dragon," he said, pointing to a bus that was roaring by. "The smoke comes out of the back."

At the big front gate of the zoo Alice saw the sign NO DOGS. Tom saw it too. He handed Alice the leash. "It's your turn to stay with Freckles, Al. Walk around to the back gate of the zoo. We'll meet you there."

Alice didn't think this was fair at all. Tom didn't like the library nearly as much as she liked the zoo. He hadn't really minded having to take the dog out of the library. But Alice wanted very much to go into the zoo.

Tom and Merlin walked down the wide steps toward the pool where the sea lions were being fed.

Alice and Freckles went down the street. Near the merry-go-round Alice sat on a bench to listen to the music. Her head began to buzz with questions.

Why did the pipe lead to the library?
Why did it disappear?

Would Merlin really be able to do magic after reading that old book?

Alice couldn't think of any answers. She got up from the bench and led Freckles into the park. The sunlight was flickering down through the leaves. Alice walked until she came to the back gate of the zoo. She looked at the statue of a mother lion playing with her cubs. It was at the top of a flight of steps.

Suddenly Alice heard the sound of running feet. Tom came rushing up the steps. He stopped when he saw his sister. "Al," he said. "I'll mind Freckles. Go down there and get Merlin. He's in the lion house, and he won't listen to me. Maybe you can do something with him."

"What's he doing?" Alice asked.

"You'll see." Tom pulled the leash away from Alice. "Hurry, Al!"

Alice ran down the steps and along the walk. She heard screams coming from a large brick building.

When Alice went into the building she saw a crowd jammed around one of the cages. An old lady had fainted, and some of the people were trying to revive her. But most of them were watching Merlin.

He had climbed over the guard rail and reached into the cage. A big lion lay on his side while the magician stroked him under the chin. The lion began to lick Merlin's hand.

The old lady opened her eyes. She

took one look at what was going on and fainted again.

A keeper with a gun put a key in the gate of the cage. "Stand back," he said to the crowd. "That lion is a mean one."

Alice was frightened, but she knew she had to do something. She pushed her way to the guard rail. "Merlin," she said, "what are you doing?"

The old man's bright blue eyes were gazing into the golden eyes of the lion. "I'm practicing," he said. "This is the first step toward regaining my power."

"Haven't you practiced enough?" Alice said, "It's lunch time. I'm hungry. And I'll bet the lion is too."

Merlin stopped stroking the lion. He climbed back over the guard rail. The people moved aside to let him pass. They seemed to be afraid of him.

Alice took the magician's hand and pulled him out of the building.

10

TOM showed Alice and Merlin a way back to the cave that cut across the hills and followed the bridle path. He took the leash off Freckles so the dog could scamper after squirrels and poke his nose into every hollow tree.

When they came to the stream, Merlin sat on a flat rock and bathed his feet in the cool water. "My feet are out of practice too," he said.

Alice wondered if the cave was gone from the bank above the stream. She looked under the vines. The old pipe was still there.

"Hey, Al," Tom yelled. "The swing is gone!"

The piece of branch Merlin had used for a seat lay on the ground. The two ropes of shining hair had disappeared.

"Some rotten kid stole the swing," Tom said. "We should have remembered you never can leave anything in the park."

Merlin didn't seem to mind. "The swing was a help to my thinking this morning. Now I don't need it. Besides, swinging tends to upset my stomach. I recall that you were talking about lunch."

It would have been easier to take the magician home with them for the meal, but Alice was afraid her mother might have the afternoon off again. "Tom," she said, "stay here with Merlin. I'll take Freckles home to feed him, and I'll bring back a picnic lunch for us. This way, if Mother or Daddy comes home, I'll have to come back to the park to get you."

Tom remembered how they had been stuck in the house yesterday afternoon. "OK," he said, "but hurry. I'm starving."

Alice was hot and tired by the time she reached home. She thought of what her mother had said about the wading pool. It would be fun to spend the afternoon in it.

She fed the dog and filled a paper bag with food — bananas, bread, potato chips, peanut butter, and three cans of cherry soda.

When Alice opened the kitchen drawer to get a knife for the peanut butter, she saw the little red flashlight her mother kept there. She knew her mother didn't want her to play with it. But Alice couldn't forget how the tunnel had disappeared when they came out of it in the library. The other end was still in the park. Alice took the flashlight out of the drawer and put it into the pocket of her jeans.

"Freckles," she said, "you look tired." The dog was stretched out on his back under the kitchen table. "I think I'll leave you at home."

Alice took the picnic lunch back to the park.

11

THE picnic was a big success. By this time Merlin was an expert at eating bananas. He finished three of them. He still didn't like the bread, but he said that peanut butter improved it. The cherry soda, Merlin said, was the finest wine he had ever tasted.

They were all three perched like birds on the split oak tree. Merlin said he'd stayed in the tree so long that he felt at home there. He sat on a twisted branch and swung his bare feet. "Such wonderful crackly things you have to eat." Merlin munched a potato chip. His blue eyes were shining, and there were crumbs in his white beard. He couldn't stop eating the potato chips until the box was empty.

When lunch was over they all climbed out of the tree and went to look for a trash basket. "There's one over near the boat house by the lake," Tom said.

Merlin stood on the stone wall at the edge of the lake and watched two boys in a pedal boat. "Marvelous!" the magician exclaimed.

Alice enjoyed the way Merlin reacted to all the new things he saw. When they were on their way back to the cave she took out the flashlight. "This is much better than a pine torch."

Merlin took the little red flashlight. Tom showed him how to click it on. They were walking under the long dark arch of the stone bridge.

Out of the shadows stepped four big boys. Alice jumped back. She saw that they were holding knives.

"Okay, old man," one of the boys

said. He poked a pointed knife at Merlin's chest. "Hand over that flashlight."

Merlin stared into the eyes of the boy who spoke to him. "What's the matter with your knife, my son?" he said in a low voice. "Look at it. It's bending."

"See how the blade droops," the magician said in the same strange clear voice. "And the handle is getting hot. In a moment it will burn you."

While Alice watched, the knife blade seemed to turn to rubber.

Merlin spoke again. "All your knives are soft and warm," he whispered. "They're getting warmer and warmer."

The boy standing in front of Alice let out a yell. He dropped his knife. When he leaned over to pick it up, Merlin said to him, "Take care. It will cut you if you touch it."

The boy reached for his knife. He

grabbed it by the blade and gashed his thumb. Now all four boys dropped their their knives and started to run. They tore out from under the bridge and raced down the walk that wound across the hills above the stream.

Tom and Alice were still under the bridge with Merlin. "Pick up the knives," the magician said softly. "You can dig a hole and bury them."

When Merlin and the children came out from under the bridge, the four boys were gone. Tom used one of the knives to dig a hole at the foot of a hawthorn tree. He dropped all the knives into the hole. Then he filled it with earth and put a large stone on top.

Alice was talking to the magician. "Is that some of the magic you got out of the library book?"

"Yes," the old man said. "Easy magic. The book helped me to remember it."

Tom had finished burying the knives. "Why did you swipe Mom's flashlight, Al?" he asked.

"I didn't swipe it," Alice said. "I only borrowed it. And I want to know what happened to the pipe when we came out of it in the library."

Tom scratched his head. "Hey, that is queer. I never stopped to think about it before. Merlin, do you feel like crawling through that pipe again?"

The magician nodded. "I was going to suggest it myself. That pipe is like an underground road. This morning I wanted more than anything to find a way to remember my magic. And the pipe led right to the book."

"You said that was easy magic you were doing." Alice took back the flashlight and put it into her pocket.

"Yes," Merlin said. "I have to have certain herbs before I can do anything difficult. And if I could find a certain charm — " The magician smiled. "But that's too much to hope for."

They had been walking along the ridge above the stream. When they came to the old split tree they crossed the stream and climbed the bank to the cave.

Alice wiggled in first. She had the flashlight. Now it was her turn to lead the way. Tom was in the middle, and Merlin crawled through last. The tunnel looked quite different by the steady beam of the flashlight. It wasn't scary at all. They went much faster than they had before. But the tunnel seemed longer than last time. Alice's knees were red and sore when at last she saw a dim light. The light got bigger and brighter. They heard water splashing.

12

THE tunnel came to an end. Alice crawled out into what seemed to be a downpour of rain. She stood up, stepped forward, and found herself standing in the sunshine. She had walked through a waterfall.

Tom came dashing through the waterfall to join her. A moment later Merlin was beside them. Alice hopped to a rocky bank and looked around. She saw a shrine near a beautiful little lake. Near it a graceful tree trailed weeping branches in the water.

"I know where we are," Tom said. "This is the botanic garden."

"Why would the tunnel lead here?" Alice asked.

Merlin stood on the gravel path and admired the view. Alice thought he might like to see the rest of the garden, as long as he was here. Besides, the tunnel had vanished again. The waterfall came out of a small pipe set in the rocks — a pipe not big enough for a water rat to crawl through.

After walking around the little lake they went to see the rose garden. Merlin had never seen such large roses. He bent over to smell one. "The little roses of long ago had more perfume," he told Alice. She thought he sounded sad, as if he were homesick for that faraway time.

"If you like to smell flowers," Alice said, "there's a special garden here for that."

"She means the Garden of Fragrance," Tom said. "You're allowed to touch the plants there."

"I would like to smell that garden," the magician told the children.

The way to the Garden of Fragrance led past the water-lily pond and the greenhouse. The magician stopped to look at the enormous goldfish swimming among the lilies. Then Tom and Alice took him into the greenhouse to show him a banana tree.

It was even hotter in the greenhouse than outside. They didn't stay there long. Alice thought again how nice it would be to splash around in the wading pool.

The Garden of Fragrance was set apart from the rest of the botanic garden by a brick wall. Tom and Alice took Merlin through the gate. The flower beds were waist high so that people could lean over to touch and smell the plants. There were all kinds of sweet-smelling herbs here.

Merlin was excited. He went from plant to plant, sniffing and touching. He broke off a few sprigs of tiny gray leaves. "Just what I need," he said. Humming to himself he walked all around the Garden of Fragrance.

Alice saw him pick some berries from a bush and slyly pull up a little plant by the roots. "Tom," she whispered, "if he keeps this up they'll make us leave the garden."

"No they won't. Look." Tom pointed.

Now Alice noticed the other people in the garden. They leaned over the plants, buried their noses in them, pulled at them. These people were blind. The Garden of Fragrance had been made for them.

"Merlin isn't acting any different from anybody else here," Tom said.

When Merlin had picked the herbs he wanted, he walked back to the children. "We can leave now," he said. "I'm ready to do difficult magic." His blue eyes twinkled. "But I don't know a spell that will make a pocket in this robe. Oh, it's a beautiful robe," he said to Alice, "but it needs a pocket."

Merlin did seem to like the bedspread. The fringe was rather soiled now. And some of the paper stars had fallen off. But the magician didn't seem to notice.

"What do you want a pocket for?" Alice asked.

"To put my herbs in," Merlin explained.

"I'll keep them in my pocket for you," Alice said. "Then, when I get home, I'll get you a plastic bag, one of those clear shiny ones you like so much."

Merlin gave Alice the leaves, roots, and berries he had gathered. She put them into the side pocket of her jeans. "We'll walk back to the cave with you," she said to the magician. "And then Tom and I must go home. I left Freckles in the house."

They walked through the turnstile that led out of the botanic garden and crossed Flatbush Avenue to get to the park.

13

MERLIN said he was going to take a nap in his cave while Alice went to get the plastic bag.

As she walked home with Tom, Alice said, "It's so hot today. Mother thought we might want to set up the wading pool. Why don't you get the parts for it out of the basement while I take the plastic bag to Merlin. Freckles can go with me for the walk."

"OK," Tom said. "But hurry back."

Alice promised to be as quick as she could. When they got home, she returned the flashlight to the kitchen drawer and took a plastic bag from the roll on the shelf. She put Merlin's herbs into the bag.

Freckles was eager to go out. Alice hooked the leash onto his collar and started back to the park.

While she was gone Tom went down into the basement. He found the parts for the wading pool in a big cardboard box under his father's workbench. Tom had to make five trips to carry all the things out to the yard.

It was a small, city backyard. A peach tree grew in one corner, and there were rosebushes all along the fence. The pool was only ten feet across and two and a half feet deep, but at least it would keep Tom and Alice cool.

Tom started to unroll the aluminum wall of the wading pool. He tried hard to set it up in a perfect circle. Then he unfolded the plastic lining. Alice came home while he was struggling to drape the lining over the wall.

"Merlin really seems to think those

herbs are important," Alice said. "I think he was afraid I wouldn't bring them back to him." She stuck her hand into her jeans pocket and took out some broken bits of leaves, roots, and berries. Alice sniffed them. "They do smell good."

The lining of the wading pool kept sliding off the wall. There were clips to hold it on, but Tom couldn't get them to grip. He was tired and hot. "Oh, Al," he said, "stop fooling with that stuff and help me." Tom grabbed the herbs and threw them into the middle of the wading-pool liner. "I wish this stupid thing would set itself up."

Instantly the wall of the wading pool gave a little shake and formed itself into a beautiful circle. The lining reached up from the ground and flapped itself over the edge of the wall. All the clips flew to their proper places and snapped the lining to the wall. Without any help from the hose, the pool started to fill with water. In a few seconds it was full.

Tom and Alice stared. For a minute Alice couldn't say a word. Then she whispered, "Tom, it must be the herbs. They *are* magic!"

"Come on, Al," Tom said. "What are we waiting for? Get into your bathing suit." He ran into the house.

Alice went into the house. She found her bathing suit in her dresser and changed into it.

When she came back into the yard Tom was already in the pool. He seemed to be swimming. Alice knew the pool wasn't deep enough for that. It was only good to splash around in. She tested the water with her toe. Usually it was too cold right after the pool was filled. The sun had to warm it for a while. Now the water was just the way Alice liked it. She stepped into the pool.

To her surprise her feet didn't touch the bottom. Alice began to swim. The water was clear and deep. She looked around. She could see a sandy beach bordered with palm trees. Tom was just ahead of her, swimming toward the beach.

The sun glinted on the water. Overhead sea birds wheeled and screamed. Alice tasted the salty brine. "Tom," she called. "Wait for me."

Tom turned around and swam back to her. He rolled over on his back and paddled in the clear water. "Isn't this great, Al?"

Alice stopped swimming and began to tread water. "That looks like an island over there. Where do you suppose we are?"

"Who cares?" Tom rolled back onto

his stomach and went on swimming toward the palm trees. Alice splashed after him.

As they came near the shore of the island the water became shallow. Alice's knees scraped on the sandy bottom. She stood up and began to wade.

Tom reached the beach before her. He stepped out of the water and turned to face Alice with a look of surprise on his face.

A moment later Alice stood beside him. She looked around. The palm trees were gone. There were the rosebushes and the tree covered with little green peaches. They were in their own back-yard.

The kitchen door opened. Mrs. Nelson came out into the yard. "I'm glad you set up the pool, children," she said. "It looks so nice and cool. I wish it was deep enough for me to go in."

14

MRS. Nelson set to work to get supper. "We're out of milk," she said. "Alice, get dressed and run to the store for me, please. Tom, see if you can find that heavy extension cord. We need it for the air-conditioner in the front bedroom."

There was no time to go back into the pool.

After supper Alice remembered that Merlin hadn't had anything to eat since lunch time. There didn't seem to be anything left from supper that she could take to him. Alice found an open box of Fig Newtons in the kitchen cabinet and a half-full container of milk in the refrigerator.

She sneaked out of the kitchen while her mother was busy wiping the top of the stove. There wasn't time to find Tom or put the leash on Freckles. Alice slipped out of the front door and ran all the way to the park.

It was not yet dark when Alice came to the meadow. She cut across it to the stream and walked around the bridge instead of going under it.

When she reached the cave she whispered through the patch of vines, "Merlin!"

There was no answer.

Alice pushed aside the vines and looked into the cave. It seemed to be bigger somehow. She poked the box of Fig Newtons and the milk under the twisted bottom bar and then wiggled under it herself.

Once she was inside the cave Alice got up on her hands and knees. She reached up and found she couldn't touch the top of the pipe. She stood up.

The floor was flat and covered with long grass-like leaves. A little fire burned in a ring of stones. Merlin was sitting at a table, drinking out of a mug. Alice saw a few bones in a wooden bowl. Merlin seemed to have been having a feast.

He was so busy drinking that he

hadn't heard Alice call him. Now he caught sight of her standing at the entrance to the cave. "Welcome," he said.

"What happened to the cave?" Alice asked. "And where did you get the food?"

"Have you forgotten the magic herbs, my child?" Merlin asked.

Alice remembered the wading pool. "You mean you just *wished* for all this?" she said. She thought for a moment. "I brought you some milk and cookies for supper, but I don't suppose you'll want them now."

Merlin wiped a drop from the side of his mouth. "The food you bring is often new to me," he said, "and often most tasty. May I see what you have?"

Alice handed him the box of Fig Newtons. The old man chose one. He looked at it closely before taking a bite.

"I don't like them much," Alice said, "but my father loves them."

Merlin chewed slowly. "I am of the same mind as your father," he said. "These little cakes make a fine ending to a meal." He put the box of Fig Newtons on a shelf which was cut into the wall.

Alice noticed that Merlin had made other changes in the cave. He had a pile of soft furry skins that looked as if they would be good to sleep on. Several strange musical instruments hung on the wall. But at the far end of his big cave the winding drainage pipe still went back into the hill.

"It's late," Alice said. "I'd better get home before my mother misses me. Good-bye, Merlin. Tom and I will be back to see you in the morning."

15

"WHERE were you, Alice?" Mrs. Nelson asked.

"I'm sorry, Mother," Alice said. "I had to take something to a friend. And I wanted to do it before it got dark."

"You should have told me you were going out," her mother said.

Alice picked up the dish towel and began to dry the dishes. "Where's Tom?"

"In the yard," Mrs. Nelson said. "I wonder what he's doing there all this time." She opened the back door. "Tom, it's time you came into the house."

"I'll get him to come in, Mother." Alice went into the yard.

She could hear the water in the wading pool lapping against the wall. Alice strained her eyes in the darkness. There was no sign of Tom.

Could he have gone back into the pool? He wasn't in his bathing suit. Alice leaned over the pool.

Suddenly a hand yanked her over the wall.

"Here's another one," a voice said.

Alice found that she was sitting in a small wooden boat. Near her a lantern gleamed. A thin man with long hair and broken teeth was rowing. Another man stood near Alice. He had a black patch over one eye and was wearing a single gold earring. Both men looked like pirates.

Now she saw Tom sitting on a coil of rope at the other end of the boat. His hands were tied behind him, and his feet were roped together.

The man near Alice scratched his

head. "Jake," he said "is this a boy or a girl?" He sounded as if he had never before seen a girl in blue jeans.

"I'm a girl," Alice said. "Why have you tied up my brother?"

"He kicked me," the pirate said.

"You were twisting my arm," Tom reminded him.

The thin man stopped rowing. "Do you want me to help you tie this one up too, Barney?"

The man with the black eye-patch scratched his head again.

"I promise I won't kick you," Alice said.

The pirate looked at her. "See that you don't!"

The boat was floating on the same bay that Alice and Tom had swum in that afternoon. The moon was rising behind the line of palm trees. She could hear the boom of the surf on the beach.

As the moon rose higher Alice saw a tall sailing ship anchored farther out in the bay. The masts and sails were dark against the night sky, but there was a glow of light from a lantern which hung in the bow of the ship.

Jake was rowing toward the ship. "What do you think these two are doing in this place? I'd have sworn we were the only ones around."

"Maybe there's another ship on the other side of that island," Barney said. "Lass, where did you come from?"

Alice didn't answer. She looked at Tom. He was dripping wet. "I fell into the pool," he explained.

The boat had come up alongside the ship. Alice and Tom looked up at the dark wooden hull. An awful smell drifted down to them.

What had seemed like a dream was turning into a nightmare. There was something horrible about the ship. Alice did not want to go aboard

Up above there was the sound of men's voices. Someone threw down a rope ladder. Barney grabbed it. "I'm going to untie you, son," he said to Tom, "and you're to climb that ladder. Mind, no more kicking."

"No more arm-twisting," Tom said.

"Agreed." The one-eyed sailor untied the ropes that bound Tom. "Up you go."

When Tom reached the deck it was Alice's turn. "I never climbed a rope ladder before," she said. Really she had always wanted to climb one, but she couldn't stand the smell of the ship.

"Get a move on," a man yelled from above.

"Don't be afraid. I'll see that you don't fall, lass." Barney lifted Alice so that her feet were on the bottom rung.

Alice grabbed the swaying ladder and

started to climb. Higher and higher she went. Her feet slipped on the ropes. The ladder banged against the side of the ship. Alice was sure she would fall off at any moment. She wondered how Tom had climbed up so fast. Would she never get to the top?

At last a sailor pulled her over the side of the ship. The horrible stench was all around. Alice felt sick from the smell. "Another one!" the sailor said. "Any more, Barney?"

The one-eyed man was climbing onto the deck. "That's all," he said.

A voice from the other end of the deck called, "What's going on over there?"

Suddenly everyone was quiet.

"It's the Captain," Barney whispered to Alice. "Mind your manners."

A tall man was walking down the deck toward them. His fingers were covered with rings that flashed in the lantern light. On his head was a cocked hat. A big sword swung by his side.

"What a charming surprise!" the Captain said. "Where did these young ones come from?"

"Barney found them floating in the bay," said the sailor who had pulled Alice onto the deck.

The Captain was still looking at Alice and Tom. "Barney," he said, "tell me about it."

The one-eyed sailor edged out of the group of men. He stood in front of the Captain. "Please, sir," he said, "Jake and me was coming back in the dingy from the island. I found the boy swimming in the water. It was no easy job to get him into the boat. We nearly capsized."

"He fought you?" the Captain asked.

"Yes, sir. We had to tie him up," Barney said.

Tom interrupted. "You're a couple of bullies. That's what you are!"

The Captain stared at Tom. "Speak when you're spoken to, boy!" he hissed.

Tom opened his mouth. Alice jabbed him with her elbow. Tom decided to be quiet.

"What about the other one, Barney?" the Captain asked.

Barney looked at Alice. "Oh, she gave us no trouble."

"Was she in the water too? She isn't wet." The Captain's eyes narrowed as he watched Barney's face.

For the first time the one-eyed sailor noticed that Alice's clothes were dry.

The Captain tapped the hilt of his sword. "Answer me," he said.

Barney trembled. "W-what?" he stammered.

"Was she in the water?" the Captain repeated.

"I — I don't really know, sir," Barney

said. "At the time I thought she was. It was dark, sir, and I saw the girl near the boat. I pulled her into it."

"Barney," the Captain said. "I hope you're not lying to me."

Poor Barney! Alice was really sorry for him. He seemed so afraid of the Captain. All the crew were afraid of him. Suddenly Alice was afraid too.

Now the Captain was staring at her. Alice wanted to run away, but there was nowhere to go. "Where are your parents, child?" The Captain asked.

Alice felt cold all over. Her mouth was dry. "I left my mother in the kitchen when I went to look for Tom. My father was somewhere else in the house."

"Then you live on the island?" the Captain said.

Alice remembered that when she and

Tom went ashore on the island they found themselves at home. She nodded in answer to the Captain's question.

He smiled again. "Take the children to my cabin. They can sleep there."

16

ALICE and Tom were both expected to sleep in the trundle bed that pulled out from under the Captain's big bed. Tom took off his wet clothes. The Captain threw him a shirt.

Alice kicked off her sneakers and slipped under the coarse blanket. The Captain left a lantern burning. When he went out he bolted the cabin door on the outside.

Tom and Alice were locked in.

They huddled together in the trundle bed. Tom whispered, "What do you think they plan to do with us?"

Alice had seen a lot of pirate movies on television. "Hold us for ransom, of course."

Tom thought about this for a while.

"Al," he said, "will they end up in our backyard if they land on the island?"

"I don't know," Alice said. "I wish Merlin were here. He'd know what to do."

"If we had the magic herbs," Tom said, "we could do something ourselves."

Alice felt in her pocket. There was not so much as a tiny leaf or stem left there. "How about the window, Tom?"

Tom ran to the small porthole. "It's too high up. And we don't have a rope ladder." He peered into the darkness. "Hey, Al, there's something going on out there."

Alice slipped out of bed and ran to the window. Looking down she could see the Captain and several men getting into the small boat.

Alice put on her sneakers. "Get dressed, Tom."

"My clothes are still wet," Tom said.

"They may get a lot wetter," Alice whispered.

Tom took off the Captain's shirt and began to struggle into his wet jeans.

Alice rolled up the shirt Tom had taken off. She stuffed it under the blanket in the trundle bed. While Tom dressed, Alice looked for more things to put into the bed. There was a pair of boots in one corner. Alice took a blanket off the big bed and used it too. When she had finished there were two rounded forms in the bed.

An old-fashioned razor was hanging on the wall. Alice used it to cut off two long locks of her brown hair. Then she went over to Tom. He was trying to tie his soggy shoelaces.

When Tom saw Alice with the razor he backed away. Tom had argued with his mother and father about his long hair. He wasn't going to let Alice cut it now.

"Please, Tom," Alice whispered. "I'll cut it where it won't show."

Tom shook his head.

Alice spread the hair she had cut from her own head across the pillow. If Tom hadn't known better he would have been sure that the lump in the trundle bed was his sister.

"See?" Alice said.

Tom stood still while Alice whacked off a lock of his red hair. She tucked it beside her own hair in the trundle bed.

"Now what?" Tom asked.

"We have to wait until someone comes." Alice put everything in the cabin the way it had been. Tom joined her in a shadowy corner near the door.

While they were waiting Alice explained her plan. They sat together in the corner for what seemed like hours. At last Tom fell asleep with his head in Alice's lap. Her head kept nodding too.

Suddenly Alice was wide awake. She heard voices and a thumping noise. The dingy had returned from the island. The pirates were coming aboard. Alice shook Tom.

The children flattened themselves against the wall. Soon they heard the bolt on the door scrape. The door was flung open, and the Captain strode into the cabin. He walked to the trundle bed and looked down at the two lumpy shapes in it. "Sound asleep," he muttered.

Like silent shadows Tom and Alice slipped out of the open door of the cabin.

17

ALICE and Tom dodged among the shadows on the deck. Tom's heart pounded, and his hands were sweating. Alice felt as if she could hardly breathe.

The sailors were busy around the main mast of the ship. The children hid behind a huge barrel. After a while the crowd of men around the mast scattered. Now Tom and Alice saw that a sailor was roped to the mast.

"Al," Tom whispered, "it's Barney."

Alice didn't know why she liked the one-eyed pirate, but she did. She couldn't leave him here with that awful Captain. Besides, Alice had a feeling that it was all her fault that Barney was in trouble. "Tom," she said, "help me untie him."

The children slipped behind the mast. "Barney," Alice whispered, "be quiet."

Tom loosened the knots at the pirate's ankles. Alice uncoiled the rope that bound his body to the mast. In a few minutes Barney stepped clear. "Make for the dingy," he said.

The three ran to the rope ladder which was still dangling over the side of the ship. One after the other they climbed down to the boat below. Barney untied the dingy from the iron ring on the ship's side. Silently in the darkness, they pushed away.

Alice took a deep breath of the fresh air. It was so good after the stench of the pirate ship.

When they had floated some distance from the ship, Barney began to row. Then Alice asked him, "What happened?"

Barney rested his oars. "The Captain

didn't find anybody on the island. He thinks I lied to him about you two. In the morning he was going to punish me. I don't want to talk about that. I've seen the Captain's punishments."

Tom said, "What will we do now?"

"Once we get to the island we'll be all right," Barney said.

"What's the island like?" Tom asked.

The pirate looked astonished. "I thought you lived there," he said.

"Tell us about it," Alice begged.

Barney started to row again. "I've never seen a place I liked so much. There are fruit trees and coconuts. And the water's full of fish. I wouldn't mind staying there for the rest of my life."

"Won't the Captain come looking for us?" Alice asked.

Barney laughed. "We've got the dingy. He'd have to swim ashore. And the Captain's no swimmer. Anyway he wants to get away from these waters. There's a fleet of warships looking for him. It's my guess he'll sail away in the morning."

The pirate rowed in silence for a while. The moon was getting low in the the sky. Barney stopped to rest. He pulled a little leather bag out of his shirt and took two gold coins out of it. He gave a coin to each of the children. "Something to remember me by," he said, "when you get back to your parents."

Alice and Tom took the coins and thanked him. Then Barney started to row again. They were getting close to the island. The trees gave off a sweet smell. When the water became shallow Barney stepped out of the boat and began to wade. He grabbed hold of the dingy to pull it onto the beach. Alice jumped to the sand.

18

THE smell from the trees changed. It was still sweet, but it was different now — like roses and peaches. Alice was in her own backyard. A moment later Tom was beside her. The island had disappeared, and so had the pirate.

The back door opened. "Alice," Mrs. Nelson called, "I thought you were going to get Tom to come into the house. It's much too late for you children to go into the pool."

All those terrible hours Tom and Alice had spent on the pirate ship had taken no time at all on the kitchen clock. Alice rubbed the gold coin to be sure it was really there.

Next morning, after Mr. and Mrs. Nelson went to work, Alice made the beds while Tom washed the breakfast dishes. Tom looked out of the kitchen window at the sparkling wading pool. The day was hot. It would be nice to splash in the cool water. But Tom's arm was still sore from being twisted and the ropes that bound him had left red welts on his wrists and ankles.

Alice came into the kitchen. "Aren't you finished yet, slowpoke?" She picked up the dishcloth and pushed Tom away from the sink.

"I want to go into the pool," Tom said, "but I'm afraid I might run into a shark this time."

"Don't you dare to even go into the yard," Alice said. "We've got to talk to Merlin. I'm sure he'll know what to do about it. Anyway, you haven't seen what he did to the cave." Alice told Tom about her visit to Merlin the night before.

"If you'd taken me along we wouldn't have run into all that trouble." Tom rubbed his arm.

Alice had finished washing the dishes. She called Freckles. The spotted dog jumped around in such excitement that Tom had to hold him for Alice to put on the leash.

The sky was blue. A blackbird sang in the top branch of a beech tree as the children raced across the meadow. They hurried along the hills above the stream. Alice saw that the stump of the old oak was sprouting tiny green shoots. The upper part of the tree had been sawed into sections and piled alongside the stump.

Merlin was sitting in the sunshine on a rock by the stream. He was just finishing a bowl of cornflakes. "Can I offer you something to eat?"

"You mean you can magic-up anything you want?" Tom asked. "I could go for an ice-cream pop."

"I'm sorry, Tom," Merlin said. "I can't offer you that. I've never seen an ice-cream pop. I can't get something by magic unless I know what it is."

Alice told Merlin about their adventures in the wading pool. He shook his head when he heard about them. "Magic is dangerous," he said. "I should never have let the herbs out of my sight. It took me years to learn how to use magic."

"Merlin," Alice said, "what can you do about the wading pool?"

"Right now," Tom said, "I want to see what Merlin did to his cave." He climbed up to the vines, pushed them aside, and wiggled into the cave. "Wow!" he said.

A candle was burning on the wooden table. Beside it was a fat book. Tom opened it. The writing in the book was very beautiful, all in red and blue and gold. But Tom couldn't read any of it. A picture of a dragon curled halfway around the margin of the page. Tom sat down on the bench.

Alice and Merlin came into the cave. "What's keeping you so long, Tom?" Alice asked. When she saw the book she sat down beside Tom and began to turn the pages.

Merlin came quickly up behind the two children and closed the book. "There are secrets in here that even I did not know," he said. "You are not yet ready for them."

"Where did you get the book?" Alice wanted to know.

"Long ago I heard about this book," the magician said. "With the magic herbs I caused it to appear."

"Maybe if I describe an ice-cream

pop you could cause that to appear," Tom said. "Can you do anything you want with the herbs?"

"No," Merlin said. "There is a charm yet more powerful. But I have never found it."

"Well, we have to do something about the wading pool," Alice said. "If we let all the water out, could we make a different enchantment?"

Merlin pulled at his beard. "I can't let anyone but myself use the herbs. I'll go with you and look at your pool."

Freckles had been nosing around in all the corners of the cave. Alice whistled for him. He came tearing out of the shadows followed by a flying mass of angry brown feathers.

Merlin waved his arms. "Stop it, Owl!" he said. "Remember your manners. The dog is a guest."

The bird flapped down onto the table

and perched on top of the book. He cocked a large yellow eye at the two children and clucked to himself.

"The owl flew into the cave last night," the magician said. "He seems to like it here."

Freckles lay on his stomach and put his spotted nose on his paws. He looked up at the bird. Alice patted his head. Slowly his tail began to wag.

Merlin looked at the bird and the dog. "There's no reason you two can't be friends." The owl gave a soft little hoot. "Now," Merlin said. "I'll take a look at your enchanted pool." He walked to the opening of the cave and lay on his stomach to slide under the bottom bar. The children followed him, and Freckles galloped after.

19

WHEN they reached the house Alice opened the front door with her key. Merlin walked into the hall. For a moment he seemed to be sniffing something. Then he nodded his head. "It's all right," he said. "There's only white magic here."

The magician went into the living room. He stopped in front of the bookcase. His eyes lit on the book of *KING ARTHUR*. Without a word Merlin pulled the book from the shelf and began to leaf through it. Near the end he started to read. His face became sad.

"What's the matter?" Alice asked.

"I wasn't around when my friends needed me," Merlin said. He put the book on the shelf and followed Alice and Tom through the house and out of the back door.

As soon as he stepped into the yard Merlin held his nose.

"What's the matter?" Tom asked.

"Keep back!" the magician said. "Something is very wrong here. I can smell it. Whatever you do, don't go near that evil pool."

Alice found it hard not to go near the pool. It seemed to pull her forward.

Merlin grabbed her arm. The plastic bag of herbs was hanging by a string around the magician's neck. He pulled out a few leaves and stems and waved them in the air while he chanted something. Then he threw the herbs into the wading pool.

As the children watched, the level of the water in the pool began to go down. In a minute the pool was empty. The sun dried the drops of water on the plastic lining. With a clatter the aluminum wall of the pool sprang open and fell to the ground. An ugly black beetle scuttled away from the fallen pool. Merlin pointed to it. "That's all that's left of the black magic here."

The big beetle dived into a flower bed and hid among the rosebushes.

Alice looked around the sunny yard. A striped yellow bee climbed out of a rose and flew away. Up in the peach tree a gray squirrel was inspecting the fuzzy little green peaches. Tom was bending over the plastic folds of the wading pool lining. "Can't you magic it back again so that it'll be safe, Merlin?" he asked.

Merlin stroked his silky beard. "I can," he said, "if you know exactly what you want."

"We really only want the wading pool to be deep enough to swim in," Alice said.

Merlin chose one of each kind of herb. He laid the sprigs in a little circle on the plastic lining of the wading pool. Then he waved his hands and spoke a few strange words.

When the last word had been said, Merlin grabbed Alice and Tom and pulled them back against the house. All the parts of the wading pool went into action at once. The aluminum wall whirled back into a circle. The plastic lining flapped into place. With a rushing sound the pool filled with water.

Merlin rubbed his hands together. "That should be what you need," he said. "Now, if you don't mind, I'd like to be getting back to my cave. I have some studying to do."

Alice and Tom took Merlin back to the park and then returned to try out the wading pool.

Alice put on her bathing suit and stepped over the rim of the pool. The water came up to her chin. Her feet rested on soft sand. A blue dragonfly flew over her head.

To her surprise Alice found that the pool was a wide lake. In the distance she could see the peach tree. Tom was standing near the back door of the house.

Alice paddled to the middle of the lake. Overhead the summer sun blazed down on Brooklyn. "Come on in, Tom," she called. "I'll race you across the pool."

20

THE next day was Saturday. Mrs. Nelson always cleaned the house on Saturday. And everybody had to help. Alice was dusting the woodwork. Mrs. Nelson scrubbed the kitchen walls. Tom was mopping the bathroom floor. Mr. Nelson went from room to room, gathering trash from the wastebaskets. He came downstairs with a big plastic garbage bag full of trash. "Alice," he said, "I found this coin on your dresser. Where did you get it?" He held up the gold coin. that the pirate Barney had given her.

Alice didn't answer. Her father put down the bag of trash. "Alice," he repeated, "where did you get this coin?"

"In the yard," Alice said.

"Are you sure?" Mr. Nelson asked. He was looking at the coin.

"Yes," Alice said. "You can ask Tom. He has one too."

Tom had finished washing the bathroom floor. He was coming downstairs with the sponge mop and pail. "What do I have too?" he asked.

"A coin like this, Tom," Mr. Nelson said. "Alice says she found it in the yard."

Tom stared at the coin. "That's right," he said, "in the yard."

"You're certain, Tom?" Mr. Nelson rubbed Alice's coin hard with his finger. He squinted at it. "Tom, I'd like to see the coin you found."

Tom pulled his pirate coin out of the back pocket of his jeans. "Here it is, Dad. I think it's a pretty old coin."

His father rubbed his chin. "I think

it's an old coin too, Tom. If it's what I think it is I'm going to dig up every inch of that yard."

Mrs. Nelson came out of the kitchen. "What's this about digging up the yard? I've just got those rosebushes growing nicely."

Mr. Nelson held up the two pirate coins. "Look at these, Jane," he said. "The children found them in the yard. I've read about the early days of Brooklyn. There were pirates coming in and out of port all the time. I think these coins came from a treasure buried right here years ago."

Mrs. Nelson looked at the coins. "Oh, George," she said, "you're such a dreamer. These are just toy money. Don't go spoiling my garden. Put those things away and let's get finished with the housecleaning."

Mr. Nelson turned the coins over and looked at the backs. "Steve Brixner collects old coins. I'll take these over to him and see what he says. If they really are old doubloons your rosebushes will have to be transplanted for a while."

Mrs. Nelson laughed. "All right," she said. "Now throw out the trash."

Tom and Alice hurried through their work. "We promised Freckles we'd take him to the park, Mom," Tom said.

"Get something to eat first." Mrs. Nelson began to set the table. "And you'd better feed Freckles or he'll really try to catch a squirrel."

On their way over to the park Alice said, "It would be awful if Daddy dug up the yard. We couldn't use the wading pool, and the peach tree would die."

"Don't worry, Al. Merlin will do something." Tom smacked his lips. "Maybe he'll change the coins to foil-wrapped chocolates."

"He'd better do it before Daddy

shows them to his friend who knows about coins." Alice pulled Freckles across the street. "Hurry, Tom."

When they reached the park the children took the leash off the dog. All three began to run. They raced across the meadow, climbed over the bridge, and hurried along the bank of the stream.

As soon as they got to the cave Freckles squeezed in and began to sniff around. Alice and Tom followed him.

It was dark in the cave. There was no sign of the magician. Freckles nosed about until he found the owl. It was asleep on a little ledge. Freckles stood on his hind legs and put his paws on

the ledge. The bird opened one eye and looked at him.

Freckles wagged his tail. Then he took his paws off the ledge. The owl went back to sleep.

"They're friends, Al," Tom said.

Alice was peering into the shadows. "I wish the owl would tell us where Merlin is."

The owl opened an eye again and hooted softly. Freckles looked up at him in the darkness and gave a bark. Then the dog raced to the back of the cave where the old pipe led back into the hill.

"Freckles seems to think Merlin went through the tunnel," Tom said. "Maybe he's gone back to the botanic garden for more herbs. Why don't we follow him?"

"We don't have a light," Alice said.

"But look at the tunnel, Al." Tom

stepped into the pipe. It was now big enough for them to stand up in. "Merlin must have been magicking it," Tom said. "Even in the dark we could follow this."

"I don't think we should take Freckles," Alice said. "Dogs aren't allowed in the botanic garden."

"We'll leave Freckles in the cave with the owl." Tom patted the dog. "You won't mind, will you, old boy?"

Freckles went back to the corner of the cave where the owl was sleeping. He lay down on the floor under the ledge and put his chin on his paws.

Alice started walking into the tunnel. "Stay close to me, Tom. I still wish we had a flashlight."

21

THE tunnel got darker until it was completely black. The children walked close together. Alice remembered how scared she'd been when Tom dropped the matches the first time they crawled through the pipe. Suddenly she remembered something. "Tom, suppose this doesn't go to the botanic garden?"

"We have to take the chance," Tom said.

The tunnel seemed longer than ever. Alice and Tom walked on and on. "Let's turn around and go back," Alice said. "We've been walking for hours."

"It only seems like hours, Al."

"Let's walk five minutes more," Alice said. "Then if we don't come to the end of the tunnel we'll go back."

"How will we know when it's five minutes?" Tom asked.

"We'll take turns counting to sixty." Alice began to count slowly, "One, two, three, four — "

Before Alice got to fifty, Tom said, "It's getting light, Al."

Alice stopped counting and strained her eyes in the darkness. Far ahead there was a faint grayness in the tunnel. The children walked faster.

At the end of the tunnel Alice and Tom walked through a doorway into a long room. Stiff statues stood all around. In a corner was a large mummy case. People were walking about, looking at things in glass cases. At the far end of the room Alice saw a barefoot figure in a long blue robe. "There's Merlin."

"But what's this place?" Tom asked. "I'm sure I've been here before. Oh, I know. It's the Brooklyn Museum!"

Alice and Tom walked over to the magician. "Hi, Merlin," Tom said.

Merlin was looking into one of the glass cases. He pointed to some pieces of blue-green stone. "Feldspar," he said.

Suddenly the lights in the museum went out. "What's the matter?" a lady asked.

Someone answered, "It must be another power failure. Everyone is using an air-conditioner today."

"It's a good thing we're only on the third floor," someone else said. "The elevators aren't running."

A man lit a cigarette lighter. The little flame glowed in the darkness. "Follow me." The man led the way to the stairway. Tom and Alice stood beside Merlin and watched the rest of the people file out of the room.

When the man with the cigarette lighter was gone, the room was dark again. Alice's eyes began to get used to the gloom. The huge statues looked spooky. She noticed that some of the things in the cases gave off a faint light.

Merlin walked from case to case. He seemed to be searching for something. For a long time he looked at a tiny bottle in the form of a woman holding a horn. Alice could see it because it glowed with a soft blue light.

Merlin stopped to stare at a piece of an old scroll. It was covered with picture writing. "A shame it isn't all here," the magician muttered. The scroll also seemed to have an inner light of its own.

Suddenly Merlin caught sight of a greenish oblong. It was some sort of openwork design, and the light from it quivered as if it were alive.

"The Eye of Horus!" the magician whispered. He pressed the diamond of his ring against the glass and cut out a

circle large enough for his hand to reach through. Merlin grabbed the greenish oblong and started to walk quickly back to where the children had come out of the tunnel.

"The tunnel won't be there," Alice said. "It never is." To her surprise the magician walked through a low archway into the drainage pipe. It was still large enough for them to stand upright. Tom and Alice ran into the opening after Merlin.

They walked through the dark pipe. "That was stealing," Alice whispered to Tom.

Merlin heard her. "The Eye of Horus belongs to no man," he said. "Whoever put it into that case had no more right to it than I do. At least I understand its value."

"What's it good for?" Tom asked.

"The whitest of white magic," the magician said.

"Maybe it can help us." Alice told Merlin about her father and the gold coins. "Tom thought you could change them into foil-wrapped chocolate coins," she finished.

"You forget that I've never seen these coins of which you speak," Merlin said.

"What is chocolate? I could change them into coins that I know."

"I don't think that would help," Alice said. "Oh, dear, what shall we do? It will be just awful if Daddy digs up the yard."

Merlin didn't answer. All three walked in silence for a while. Alice was thinking of the wide lake with the blue dragonflies. Her father would never believe her if she told him about it. She wondered if Tom would mind as much as she did not being able to use the wading pool. Then he said, "Gee, Al, it was such fun being able to race in that pool. And I even swam underwater yesterday. There were minnows down there."

The tunnel began to get light. In a few minutes Merlin and the children stepped into the cave. Freckles was still waiting near the owl.

22

ALICE and Tom had never seen Merlin so excited. His eyes were shining and his bare feet skipped across the floor of the cave. He held the Eye of Horus up and almost danced. "I can go home now," he said.

"What do you mean, Merlin?" Tom asked. "Aren't you happy here?"

"I don't really belong here," the magician said. "I'm going back through time to where my friends need me."

"But we need you too, Merlin," Tom said. "Aren't you going to change the coins for us?"

"I'm afraid I can't," Merlin said. "But touch the Eye of Horus for luck."

Tom stepped forward and touched

the green oblong. He gave a little start and jumped back from it.

"You too, Alice," the magician said.

Alice gently touched the beautiful old charm. It seemed to vibrate beneath her fingers. Alice felt as if a faint electric shock had run through her whole body.

"We have to go now," she told the magician. "Good-bye."

She and Tom slipped under the twisted bar. Freckles came after them.

Merlin called good-bye to the children through the leafy vine. Tom and Alice slid down the bank to the stream. They crossed over on the stones and hurried toward home.

Mrs. Nelson was waiting for them. She looked as if she had been crying.

"What's the matter, Mother?" Alice asked.

"It's your father," Mrs. Nelson said. "He's found out that those coins really are old Spanish doubloons. He says if there are more of them buried in the yard we'll be rich. I don't want to be rich. Can't you persuade him not to dig up the yard?"

"Where is Daddy?" Tom asked his mother.

"In the yard," Mrs. Nelson said.

Tom ran through the house and out of the back door. Mr. Nelson had unrolled the hose and was getting ready to siphon the water out of the wading pool. "Stop, Daddy!" Tom screamed.

Alice came out of the house too. When she saw what her father was doing, she ran over to him and touched his arm. "Daddy, please!"

The instant Alice touched him Mr. Nelson seemed to give a little shiver. An ugly black beetle ran out of the garden bed. Alice's father stepped on it.

He rubbed his forehead and looked

at the children. Then he put down the hose. "I don't know what came over me," he said, "to want to dig up your mother's rosebushes. Did you really find those coins here in the yard?"

"Not exactly," Alice admitted. "A man gave them to us. We helped him when he was in trouble."

"Why didn't you tell me before?" Mr. Nelson asked.

"You always told us not to take things from strangers," Alice said. "I was afraid you'd be angry. I'm sorry, Daddy."

"Well, I'll keep these coins for you and Tom until you're older," Mr. Nelson said. "And next time you want to lie about something remember how much trouble it can cause."

Tom and Alice spent the rest of the afternoon in the pool. Their mother and father sat on a bench under the peach tree. "Who could believe that a little pool could be so much fun for the children?" Mrs. Nelson said. "Aren't you glad you didn't let the water out?"

Mr. Nelson was watching Tom. "He almost seems to be swimming. But of course that pool is only deep enough to wade in."

After supper, before it got dark, Tom and Alice took Freckles to the park. They made their way to the cave.

"We have to thank Merlin," Alice said. "It was my touching the Eye of Horus and then touching Daddy that did the trick."

Tom was first up the bank. He pulled aside the vines. "Al," he said, "look!"

The twisted bar had been replaced by a shiny new one. There was no longer any way to get into the cave. The children looked through the bars. The big cave was gone. There was just an empty drainage pipe going back into the hill.